The Jealousy Man

I glanced out at the plane's wing. Beneath us, bathed in sea and sunshine, lay a sandy-coloured island. Kalymnos.

The captain warned us we might be in for a rough landing and I closed my eyes and leaned back in my seat. Ever since I was a child I have known I was going to fall from the sky into the sea and drown. I can even recall the day this truth came to me.

My father worked for the family firm of which his older brother, Hector, was head. We children loved Uncle Hector because he always brought presents when he came to see us, and let us ride in his car, the only open-top Rolls-Royce in all Athens. My father usually returned from work after I had gone to bed, but that evening he was early. He looked worn out and after tea he had a long phone conversation with my grandfather in his study. I could hear that he was very angry. When I went to bed he sat on the edge and I asked him to tell me a story.

He told the tale of Icarus and his father. They lived in Athens, but they were on the island of Crete when his father, a wealthy craftsman, made wings from feathers and wax with which he was able to fly. People were very impressed by this and when the father gave the wings to Icarus, he urged his son to fly exactly as he had done. But Icarus was so thrilled at finding himself so high above the ground, that he forgot that it wasn't his own ability that let him fly but the wings his father had given him. So he flew higher than his father. Icarus came too close to the sun and the wax that held the wings melted. He fell into the sea and drowned.

As I was growing up, it seemed to me that my father's version of the Icarus myth was meant as a warning. Uncle Hector was childless and it was thought I would succeed him. Not until I was grown up did I learn that, at around that time, the firm had almost gone bankrupt. This was because of Hector's reckless gambling on the price of gold, and my grandfather had fired him. To avoid public disgrace he allowed him to keep his title and office.

My father then ran the firm and ever since that bedtime story I have had nightmares of falling and drowning. My father was warning me not to take foolish risks. Actually, on some nights the dream seems like something pleasant, a sleep in which everything painful ceases to exist.

The Greek flag was blowing straight out from the flagpole by the little terminal building as we left the plane, and I heard the pilot say to the stewardess that the airport had just closed.

In the terminal a man wearing a blue police uniform stood in front of the luggage belt and studied the passengers. As I headed towards him he gave me a questioning look and I nodded.

'George Kostopoulos,' he said, holding out a large hand. 'Thank you for coming at such short notice, Inspector Balli.'

'Call me Nikos,' I said.

'Sorry I didn't recognise you, but there aren't many pictures of you, and I thought you were older.'

I had inherited from my mother looks that don't age much with the years and, although my hair was grey, I had kept a fighting weight of seventy-five kilos.

'You don't think fifty-nine is old enough?'

'Well, of course.' He smiled beneath a moustache of the type men in Athens had shaved off twenty years earlier. But his eyes were mild and I knew I wouldn't be getting any trouble from George Kostopoulos.

'It's just that I've been hearing about you ever since I was at the Police Academy, and that seems like a long time ago to me. Any more baggage?'

'Only this hand baggage,' I said.

'We've got Franz Schmid, the brother of the missing man, at the station in Pothia,' said George as we crossed to a small, dust-coated Fiat.

'I read the report,' I said, putting my bag on the back seat. 'Has he said anything else?'

'No, he's sticking to his story. His brother Julian left their room at six in the morning and never returned.'

'It said Julian went for a swim?'

'That's what Franz says.'

'But you don't believe him?'

'No. I would have if he and Julian had not had a fight the previous evening, in front of witnesses.'

We turned down a narrow track with bare olive trees and small white stone houses on both sides. 'They just closed the airport,' I said. 'I suppose that's because of the wind.'

'It happens all the time,' said George. 'That's the trouble with having the airport on the highest point of an island.'

I could see what he meant. As soon as we got between the mountains the flags hung limply down from the flagpoles.

'Fortunately my evening flight leaves from Kos,' I said. The secretary in the Homicide Department had checked before my boss had allowed me to make the trip. Even though we give extra care to the very few cases involving foreign tourists, I was to spend only one working day on it. Usually I was given more time, but even the legendary Detective Inspector Balli was subject to budget cuts. And as my boss put it, this was a case with no body, no media interest and no reasonable grounds to suspect a murder.

There were no return flights from Kalymnos in the evening, but there was one from Kos, a forty-minute ferry ride from Kalymnos, so he had grunted his assent.

'I'm afraid the boats to Kos won't be going either in this weather,' said George.

'This weather? The sun is shining and there's hardly a breath of wind except up there.'

'I know it seems unlikely, but there's a stretch of open sea before you reach Kos and there have been a number of accidents in weather just like this. We'll book a hotel room for you. Maybe the wind will have eased off by tomorrow.'

I thought of the few contents in my bag, but perhaps I might be able to get a little well-earned rest here. I'm the type who has to be forced to take a holiday, even when I know I need one.

Maybe being both childless and wifeless is what makes me so bad at holidays. They feel like a waste of time and make me feel lonely.

'What's that?' I asked, pointing. Surrounded by steep slopes lay what looked like a village carved from grey rock. But there were no signs of life.

'Paleochora,' said George. 'In the twelfth century, if the people of Kalymnos spotted enemy ships they would flee up there and barricade themselves in. People also hid there during the Second World War when the Allies bombed Kalymnos because it was being used as a German base.'

'So a must-see,' I said.

'Hm,' said George. 'Actually no. It looks better from a distance. It's overgrown, there's rubbish, goats, and the chapels are used as toilets.'

But I was, of course, tempted. I always find myself tempted by what rejects me, shuts me out. Women. Human conduct. Murder cases. All the things I don't understand.

Pothia was a town of narrow one-way streets and alleys. Even though it was nearly November, and the tourist season had ended, the streets were crowded. We parked outside a two-storey house in the harbour area where fishing boats and luxurious yachts lay alongside one another. A small ferry was moored to the quayside and a group of foreign tourists were discussing something with a man in a naval uniform.

Some of the tourists had rucksacks with coils of rope sticking out from the top flap. Climbers. Over the last fifteen years, Kalymnos had changed from being a sun-and-surf island to a place for sport climbers; but by then I had given up climbing. The man in the naval uniform spread his arms wide to protest that there was nothing he could do.

There were white crests but the waves weren't dangerously high.

'The problems arise further out, you can't see from here,' said George, who had read the look on my face.

'That's often the case,' I said with a sigh.

George entered the police station ahead of me, and I nodded greetings left and right as we walked through a crowded open-plan office where both the furniture and the bulky computer screens seemed outdated.

'George!' called a woman stepping out from her desk. She looked to be about thirty, small and athletic-looking in a uniform with the white ribbon of the tourist police. 'A journalist from *Kathimerini* rang. They want to know if we've arrested the brother of the missing man. I told them I would ask you to ring them.'

'Call them yourself, Christine. Say there have been no arrests and that at this moment we have no comment.'

I understood. George wanted to work in peace, and Franz Schmid had made himself available for questioning. He was not under arrest. To avoid rumours it was best to say that the police were talking to anyone who could give them a clearer picture of what might have happened, and that included the missing man's brother.

George stopped in front of a door. 'Franz Schmid's in there.'

'OK,' I said. 'Has the word "lawyer" been mentioned yet?'

George shook his head. 'We asked if he wanted to call the embassy but he said, "What can they do to help find my brother?"'

'Does that mean you haven't told him that he's a suspect?'

'I asked him about the fight, that's all. But he probably realises we've asked him to wait here until you come for a reason.'

'And who did you say I was?'

'A specialist from Athens.'

'Specialist in what? Finding missing persons? Or finding killers?'

'I didn't specify, and he didn't ask, Nikos.'

*

The room I stepped into was about three metres by three. The only light came from two narrow windows high up on one wall. A tall man was sitting at a small table on which stood a jug of water and a glass. Both his forearms were resting on the blue-painted wooden tabletop. He was slender, with a face aged beyond his twenty-eight years, wearing a cap with stripes in Rastafarian colours and a little skull on the rim. Dark curls poked out from beneath the cap. The eyes were so deep-set I couldn't immediately read anything in them.

It dawned on me that there was something familiar here, but it took me a second to remember. It was a photo of the singer Townes Van Zandt on the cover of a record Monique had in her room in Oxford. Townes Van Zandt is sitting at a similar table, posed in almost the same way. He has a similarly blank face that still seems sensitive because it's so naked and exposed.

'*Kalimera*,' I said to test his Greek.

'*Kalimera*,' he replied.

'Not bad, Mr . . .' I glanced at the folder I had taken from my bag. 'Franz Schmid. Does that mean you speak Greek?' I asked in my very British English, and he gave the expected reply.

'Unfortunately no.'

I hoped that with my question I had set up

11

our starting point. That I knew nothing about him and he could, if he wanted to, change his story for this new listener.

'My name is Nikos Balli, I am an inspector from the Homicide Department in Athens. I am here, I hope, to remove any suspicion that your brother has been the victim of a crime.'

'Is that what you think has happened?' The question was asked in a straightforward way.

'I have no idea what the local police think and at this moment I don't believe anything. What I do know is that murders are rare in Greece. But any murder is so harmful to the country's appeal as a holiday destination that when one does happen, we have to show the world that we take it very seriously. So I might ask you about details which may seem annoying and pointless to someone who has recently lost his brother.

'It might also sound as though I believe that you or others killed him. But it is simply my task to test the idea that a murder may have been committed. It will be a success if I am able to dismiss that thought, and we might be a step closer to finding your brother. All right?'

Franz Schmid gave a small smile that didn't quite reach to his eyes. 'You sound like my grandfather.'

12

'Sorry?'

'You take the scientific approach. Programming of the object. He was one of the German scientists who fled Hitler and helped the USA develop the atom bomb. We . . .' He stopped. 'I'm sorry, I'm wasting your time, Inspector. Fire away.'

Franz Schmid's gaze met mine. When he said 'programming of the object' he was clearly referring to the fact that I had given him a reason to help me – that it might help us to find his brother. In other words, programming him, the object in this case. It was a standard trick. But I suspected that Franz Schmid had also spotted the hidden trick I had used, to get him to lower his guard. I had almost apologised in advance for the tough tone of what was to follow and had blamed the Greek tourist industry. This was to make me appear to be the decent, honest cop in whom Franz Schmid could safely confide.

As I listened to his story, Franz Schmid's body language didn't tell me much. He seemed patient and he told his story calmly. But the guilty are often more convincing than the innocent. They have a story ready, whereas the innocent tell the story as it comes to them. So body language was a secondary issue for me. *Stories* are my speciality.

There were other clues. Such as that Franz

Schmid, although clean-shaven, seemed to be a type of hipster, the type that wears a cap and a thick flannel shirt indoors even when it's hot. The sleeves of the shirt were rolled up and his bare forearms seemed very muscular. The watch on his left wrist was a Tissot T-Touch which had a barometer and an altimeter. In other words, Franz Schmid was a climber.

According to the case notes, Franz and Julian Schmid were Americans, living in San Francisco, unmarried, with Franz working for an IT firm and Julian for a well-known producer of climbing equipment.

Franz Schmid told me he had woken at six in the morning in the room he and his brother had rented in a house by the beach in Massouri, a town about a fifteen-minute drive from Pothia. Julian was about to go out to swim the eight hundred metres to the island of Telendos, something he did every morning. On this day he never came back.

Franz went to the stone jetty below the house. His brother's towel lay at the end, with a stone to stop it blowing away. It was dry. Franz ran back up to the house and got the landlord to ring the police.

First on the scene were the mountain rescue team, who at once got two boats out on the water and began the search. Next came the divers. And finally the police. They got Franz to check that none of Julian's clothes were missing and checked that Julian could not have gone to his room unseen by Franz, dressed and left the house.

After searching the beach, Franz and some of his climbing friends rented a boat and crossed over to Telendos. They visited the houses on the mountainside there, asking if anyone had seen a swimmer come ashore.

After returning from the failed search, Franz spent the rest of the evening calling family and friends to tell them that Julian was missing. He hardly slept, and at daybreak the police telephoned and asked if he could come to the station to assist them. And that was – Franz Schmid looked at his Tissot watch – eight and a half hours ago.

'The fight,' I said. 'Tell me about the fighting the night before.'

Franz shook his head. 'It was a stupid quarrel. We were in a bar playing billiards. We were all a bit drunk. Julian started shooting his mouth off and I had a go back at him. Next thing I know I've thrown a billiard ball at him and hit him on the head. Down he went, and when he came to he started throwing up. I thought he had concussion, so I drove him to the hospital in Pothia.'

'Do you often fight?'

'When we were kids, yeah. Now, no.' He rubbed the stubble on his chin. 'We didn't reach the hospital. Julian insisted he was feeling better and that we should turn round. He said that if we were stopped by the police they'd suspect me of drink driving, I'd end up in a cell and he wouldn't have anyone to climb with. So we drove back.'

'Did anyone see you come back?'

'Someone must have. We parked on the main road, where all the restaurants are, and there are always people there.'

'Good. Did you meet anyone who can confirm this?'

Franz took his hand away from his chin. 'We didn't meet anyone we know. And it was fairly quiet. In the autumn it's mostly climbers in Massouri, and climbers go to bed early.'

'So no one saw you.'

Franz sat up straight. 'Inspector, what has this to do with my brother going missing?' His voice was still calm, but for the first time I saw something that might have been tension in his face.

'I'm pretty sure you can work it out for yourself.' I nodded towards the folder on the table. 'It says that the landlord was woken by the sound of loud voices coming from your room, and he

16

heard chairs being dragged about. Were you still quarrelling?'

I saw a slight twitch pass across Franz Schmid's face.

'We weren't exactly sober,' he said quietly. 'But we were friends by the time we fell asleep.'

'What were you quarrelling about?'

He took hold of the glass of water in front of him as though it were a lifebelt. He drank. I knew what he was thinking: that, if I didn't get the truth from him, then I would get it from witnesses. What he didn't know was that George Kostopoulos had already learned about the quarrel from a witness. That this was what caused George to ring the Homicide Department in Athens. And why it had ended up on my desk. The Jealousy Man's desk.

'A dame,' said Franz.

'Whose dame?' I asked.

A slight smile. 'That's exactly what the shouting was about.'

'Can you give me the details, Franz?'

I had used his forename, which is an efficient way of creating a bond with someone you're questioning. And now I gave him the look that gets murder suspects to open their hearts to the Jealousy Man.

*

17

The murder rate in Greece is low. So low that a lot of people wonder how it's possible in a crisis-ridden country with so many poor people and so much corruption. The smart answer is that rather than kill someone they hate, Greeks allow the victim to go on living in Greece. Another is that we don't have organised crime because we're unable to get organised. But of course we have blood that is capable of boiling.

And I'm the man they call in when there's a suggestion that jealousy is the motive behind a murder. They say I can smell jealousy. That's not true of course. Jealousy has no smell. But it has a story. And it's listening to this story that tells me whether I am sitting with a helpless, wounded animal. I listen and know, because it is me, Nikos Balli, I am listening for. Because I am myself a wounded animal.

And Franz told me his story because this bit of the truth is always good to tell. To get it out and air the defeat and hate that are the story's natural result. For there is nothing twisted in wanting to kill whatever might stand in the way of our primary human function which is to mate, to have children so as to pass on our unique genes. It is the opposite that is twisted – allowing ourselves to be stopped in this by what is known as morality, the rules put in place to allow the community to live together in peace.

On one of their rest days from climbing, Franz had rented a moped and ridden to the village of Emporio where he met Helena, who worked as a waiter in her father's restaurant. He fell hard for her. Three dates and six days later they became lovers in the ruins of Paleochora. They were discreet; but Franz told his brother, showed Julian a video of her sitting on the castle wall.

Since childhood they had shared every tiny detail of their lives, so that all experiences became shared experiences.

'I was so much in love with Helena that I couldn't think or talk about anything else. So maybe it wasn't surprising that Julian was attracted to Helena too. And fell in love.'

'Without ever having met her?'

Franz nodded. 'I didn't think he'd ever met her. I had told Helena I had a brother, but not that we were identical twins. Then, three days ago, my phone went missing. It was the only place I had Helena's number and she and I exchanged text messages all the time. She must be thinking I was through with her.

'I made up my mind to drive to Emporio the next day, but the next morning I heard a phone vibrating in the pocket of Julian's jacket while he was out swimming. It was a text message from Helena, thanking him for a nice evening and hoping they could meet again soon. And I realised what had happened.'

He noticed my – probably badly acted – puzzled look. 'Julian had taken *my* phone,' he said, sounding almost cross. 'He found her number and called her on my phone so she thought it was me when she saw the caller ID. They arranged to meet and, even after they met, she didn't realise that the person wasn't me but Julian.'

'Aha,' I said.

'I demanded to know the truth when he returned and he admitted everything. I was furious, so I went off climbing with some other people. We didn't meet again until the evening, at that bar, and Julian claimed that he'd called Helena, told her the truth, and that she'd forgiven him for tricking her. He said that they were in love with each other. I was furious and we started arguing again.'

I nodded, thinking that Franz's jealousy was so intense that—

My thoughts were cut off by a guitar riff I knew well. 'Black Dog' by Led Zeppelin. Franz Schmid turned and took a phone from a pocket of the jacket hanging on the wall behind him. He studied the display as the riff went into the bit where John Bonham's drums and Jimmy Page's guitar just don't go together, and yet do so perfectly.

Franz Schmid held the phone to his ear.

'Yes?' He listened. 'One moment.' He held the phone out to me.

I took it.

'Inspector Balli,' I said.

'This is Arnold Schmid, uncle to Frank and Julian,' said a harsh voice. 'I am a lawyer. I would like to know on what grounds you are holding Franz.'

'We are not holding him, Mr Schmid. He wished to assist us in the search for his brother, and we are accepting his offer as long as it remains open.'

'Put Franz back on the line.'

Franz listened for a while, then placed the phone on the table between us with his hand on top of it. He told me he was tired, that he wanted to get back to the house, but that we were to call him if anything turned up.

'The phone,' I said. 'Do you mind if we take a look at it?'

'I gave it to the policeman I was talking to. With the PIN code.'

'I don't mean your brother's phone. I mean yours.'

'Mine?' His hand tightened like a claw around the phone. 'Er, will this take long?'

'Not the actual phone,' I said. 'What I'm asking for is formal permission to look at the call log and text messages that have been registered on your phone over the last ten days. All we need is for you to sign a standard release form to obtain the records from the telephone company.' I smiled as though it was awkward but necessary. 'It will help me to cross your name off the list of possible leads we need to follow.'

Franz Schmid looked at me sharply. As when a chess opponent makes an unexpected move.

It was as though I could feel the thoughts racing through his head.

He'd been ready for us to want to check his phone, so he'd deleted the calls and text messages he didn't want us to see. But maybe nothing got deleted at the telephone company? Shit! I could see him think. He could, of course, refuse. But how would it look if he made things difficult? I saw what looked like panic in his eyes.

Then, 'Of course,' he said. 'Where do I sign?'

His brain had scanned the messages. Nothing crucial there, probably. But for one revealing moment he had lost his poker face.

*

'Well?' said George Kostopoulos. He was at his desk in the open-plan office.

'The suspect is on his way back to Massouri,' I said, handing him the sheet of paper with Franz Schmid's signature. 'And I'm afraid he suspects that we're on to him and could do a runner.'

'No danger of that. The forecast is for the wind to increase. Are you saying that you . . . ?'

'Yes. I think he killed his brother. Can you mail me the records as soon as you get them from the telephone company?'

'Yes. Shall I ask them to send Julian Schmid's text messages and call logs too?'

'I'm afraid that requires a court order so long as he's not confirmed dead. But you've got his phone?'

'Sure,' said George.

I took Julian's phone and browsed through the call logs and text messages. Nothing of relevance to the case.

I jumped as the phone began to vibrate in my hand at the same time as a male voice started singing. I took a deep breath and pressed ACCEPT.

'Julian?' whispered a female voice.

'This is the police,' I said in English.

'Sorry,' said the female voice. She sounded sad. 'I was hoping it might be Julian, but . . . any news?'

23

'Who is this?'

'Victoria Hässel. A climbing friend. I didn't want to bother Franz and . . . yeah. Thanks.'

She hung up and I took a note of the number. 'That ringtone,' I said. 'What was it?'

'No idea,' said George.

'Ed Sheeran,' came Christine's voice from the other side of the room. ' "Happier".'

'Thanks,' I called back.

'Anything else we can do?' asked George.

'Yes. He was drinking from a glass in there. Can you get it finger-printed? And test for DNA if there's any saliva on the rim.'

George cleared his throat. I knew what he was going to say. That this would require a court order.

'I suspect the glass might have been at a crime scene,' I said.

'Sorry?'

'If, in the DNA report, you don't link the DNA to a named person but simply to the glass, the date and the place, that'll be OK. It might not be allowed in court, but it could be useful for you and me.'

George raised one of his thick eyebrows.

'That's the way we do it in Athens,' I lied. The truth is that sometimes that's the way *I* do it in Athens.

*

24

It was seven in the evening and I was lying on the bed in the hotel room in Massouri. High above me on the other side of the road, yellow-white limestone rock rose up. It was beautiful and inviting in the moonlight. On the other side of the hotel the mountainside plunged straight down into the sea.

The second day of searching the waters between Kalymnos and Telendos was over. Given the forecast for tomorrow, there wasn't going to be a third day. In any event, when someone is believed to have been lost at sea, the search is limited to two days. The wind rattled the windows and I could hear the waves breaking against the rocks.

My task – to decide whether jealousy was a motive for murder – was over. I wasn't good at the next step, the finding of facts. My colleagues from Athens would take care of that. Now the weather had delayed that happening and it exposed my failings as a homicide detective.

My chief said although I had high emotional intelligence, I lacked practical imagination. That's why he called me the jealousy investigator. It was why I was sent in as a scout and pulled out as soon as I had given the case the red or green light.

There's something called the eighty per cent

25

rule in murder cases. In eighty per cent of cases the guilty party is closely related to the victim. In eighty per cent of those cases the guilty party is the husband or boyfriend. And in a further eighty per cent of these the motive is jealousy. It means that there's a fifty-one per cent chance that a 'murder' motive is jealousy. This is what makes me an important man.

I learned to read other people's jealousy when I realised that Monique was in love with someone else. I went through all the agonies of jealousy, from disbelief and despair, to rage, self-contempt and finally depression. And I learned that although the pain filled me, it was like seeing myself from the outside.

It was like being a patient without pain relief lying on the operating table and at the same time watching from the gallery above while a person has his heart cut out. I was damaged by that, but it made me immune. I can never again feel jealousy, not in that way.

Does that also mean I can never love anyone again? I really don't know. Maybe there were other things in my life besides jealousy that led to my never having felt the same about anyone as I felt about Monique. On the other hand, she made me what I have become in my working life. The Jealousy Man.

I am able to understand a person's probable motive because I have been there myself. Our jealousy makes us similar and our behaviour becomes similar, in the way drug addicts behave in similar ways. We are all of us like the living dead in movies, who rave through the streets driven by a single need. To fill the black hole that is inside us.

I fell asleep and dreamed of falling from a great height. And woke an hour later.

I had mail on my phone. It was Franz Schmid's deleted messages and call logs. The night before his brother went missing he had called Victoria Hässel eight times. She had not replied. The feeling of someone hitting the ground from a great height didn't come until I read the text message Franz had sent to Helena Ambrosia.

I have killed Julian.

Emporio was a tiny hamlet at the north end of Kalymnos. The girl who came to my restaurant table reminded me of Monique. This girl was pretty too. Slim, long-legged, graceful. Brown, soft eyes. But her skin was not good and she had no chin. What was it Monique lacked? I could no longer remember. Decency, maybe.

'How can I be of service, sir?'

'Are you Helena Ambrosia?'

27

She nodded. I introduced myself and explained that I was there to talk about the missing Julian Schmid. And I saw the worry that spread across her face as I told her what I knew of her meetings with Franz Schmid. She and I were the only ones in the restaurant, but she glanced over her shoulder to make sure no one overheard us.

'Yes, yes, but what does this have to do with the one who's missing?' she whispered, angry and pink with shame.

'You've been with them both.'

'What? No!' She raised her voice, then lowered it once more to an angry whisper. 'Who says so?'

'Franz. You met his twin brother Julian in the stone city, Paleochora, when Julian pretended he was Franz.'

'Twin?'

'Identical,' I said.

'But . . .' I could see her running through the events in her head, see her confusion change to disbelief and change again to outrage.

'I've . . . I've been with two brothers?' she stammered.

'Didn't you know?'

'How could I? If there really are two of them then they're exactly alike.' She pressed her hands to her temples as though to stop her head exploding.

'So Julian was lying when he told his brother he phoned you on the day after you met him in the stone city? Told him he'd explained everything to you, and said that you forgave him?'

'I haven't spoken to either one of them since that day!'

'What about that message you got from Franz. "I have killed Julian."'

She blinked. 'I didn't understand that message. Franz had not told me his brother's name. When I read the text I thought maybe Julian was the name of a route he'd climbed – the climbers give them names, you know. We had just closed and I was very busy clearing up, so all I did was send a smiley in reply.'

'All the texts you sent to Franz are short answers to long messages. The text you sent the morning after you met Julian is the only one where you wrote first, the only one where I notice, on your side, a certain . . . affection?'

She bit her lip. Nodded. Her eyes brimmed with tears.

'So it wasn't until you met Julian that you fell in love?'

'I . . .' All the energy seemed to drain from her and she slumped into a chair opposite me. 'When I met . . . the one called Franz, I was very excited. And flattered, I guess. We met at Paleochora, where there are hardly ever any people. The last time I let him kiss me goodnight, even though I wasn't in love, not really. So when he – no, that must have been Julian – texted me and asked to see me, I said no.

'But,' she went on, 'he wrote in a way he'd never done before. He was sweet and funny. So I agreed to a final meeting. And when we met at Paleochora it was as though everything had changed. Him, me, the way we talked together, the way he held me. He was so much more relaxed and playful and we laughed a lot more. I just thought it was because we had got to know each other better.'

'Did you and Julian have sex?'

'We . . .' Her face flushed. 'Do I have to answer?'

'You don't have to answer anything at all, Helena, but the more I know, the easier it will be for me to solve the case.'

'And find Julian?'

'Yes.'

She closed her eyes. 'Yes, yes, we did. And it was very good. When I went home that evening, I knew that I had been wrong, that I was in love and that I had to see him again. And now he's . . .'

Helena buried her face in her hands. A sob came from behind the fingers. Fingers that were long and thin, like Monique's – Monique who used to hold up her fingers and say they looked like spider's legs.

I asked Helena a few more questions which she answered without hiding anything. She had the lover's freedom from shame, in the belief that love rises above all else. Now it had turned into the worst form of torture. It had been held out to her, and as quickly taken away. By the time I left she was crying again.

'Victoria.' The voice sounded out of breath.

'Nikos Balli, I'm a detective,' I said. 'We spoke on Julian Schmid's phone. There are a few questions I'd like to ask you.'

'I'm on the peak right now. Can it wait?'

'Which peak?'

'It's called Odysseus.'

'I'll come there.'

Twenty minutes later I stood on a track on a bare mountainside where a couple of thyme plants were all that grew. I wiped the sweat from my brow and looked up at a rock face about a hundred metres wide and some forty to fifty metres high. It cut across the hillside like a wall. Spread out along the base of the wall I saw at least twenty ropes that ran between the anchors on the ground and the climbers on the wall.

This type of climbing goes something like this: before the team of two starts out, the one who's climbing first attaches one end of the rope to his harness, which also holds the number of metal links called carabiners that he's going to need on the route. Metal bolts have been spaced across the route and fastened to the rock. When the climber reaches one of these, he fastens a carabiner to the bolt and then fastens the rope to the carabiner.

The second member of the team, the anchor on the ground, has a rope lock fastened to his climbing harness and the rope runs through this lock in much the same way as the seat belt in a car runs between rollers.

The anchor carefully lets out the rope as the climber goes up, the way you have to pull out a car safety belt slowly so that it doesn't lock. Should the climber fall, the rope is pulled so swiftly that the lock clamps over the rope. So if the climber falls, he won't fall far beyond the last carabiner to which he fastened the rope, and will be stopped there by the lock and the body weight of the anchor.

It is fairly free from danger, compared with free solo climbing, where you climb without ropes. All the same, nothing is completely safe.

I walked the last few metres to the wall and

found the ledge where a woman stood holding a rope that ran up to a climber ten metres above her. I scrambled up to her.

'Victoria Hässel?' I asked, panting.

'Welcome aboard,' she said without taking her eyes off the climber.

I held on tight to a deep crack in the wall, leaned out cautiously and peered down.

'Afraid of heights?' asked Victoria Hässel. She still hadn't looked at me as far as I could tell.

'Isn't everybody?' I asked. 'Some more than others.'

I looked up at her climbing partner who was a boy quite a bit younger than her. Judging by his footwork he had more to learn.

It was hard to judge Victoria Hässel's age – anything from thirty-five to forty-five. She looked strong. She was almost skinny, with long legs and a muscular back. She had chalk on her hands and was wearing climbing breeches.

She had given my suit and brown leather shoes a disapproving look. I could feel my hair being blown about in the wind. Her own was held under a knitted cap.

'A lot of climbers,' I said with a nod towards the wall.

'Usually more,' said Victoria. 'But there's too much wind today, so a lot of people are sitting in the cafes.' She nodded towards the white-whipped sea.

From here we had a view of the main road, the cars, Massouri centre. The people looked like ants down there. Along the bare hillside below us I could see climbers coming along the track.

'What's this about, Mr Balli?' Victoria asked.

'Oh, that can wait until your climber is down.'

'It's an easy one. Go ahead, talk.'

'Fair enough,' I said. 'But can I point out that your climber just clipped the rope the wrong way round onto that last carabiner?'

Victoria Hässel looked sharply at me, then looked up at the carabiner and saw I was right. If he fell, the rope could slip out of the carabiner and he would keep on falling.

'I saw that,' she lied. 'Any moment now he'll hook the rope into the next carabiner and then he'll be secure.'

I coughed. 'Looks like the hardest bit, the crux, is coming up now. It might give him trouble. If he falls and the carabiner doesn't take the weight, then the next one's so low it won't stop him before he hits the ground. Agree?'

'Alex!' she shouted.

'Yes?'

'You've clipped the last carabiner wrongly. Climb down and clip it on properly!'

'I think I better carry on up to the next bolt and clip on the right way there,' he shouted back.

'No, Alex, don't . . .'

But he had already moved away from the good fingertip holds and was on his way up to a large, downward-sloping hold. It probably looked good to him but, to the trained eye, it had too much chalk over it from where climbers before him had tried and failed to get a hold.

His trouser legs flapped. Not because of the wind but because of the stress reaction climbers call the 'sewing machine'. Sooner or later it affects everybody. I watched as Victoria took in as much of the rope as she could to make it as short as possible, but it was too little and we both knew Alex would hit our shelf.

Alex's elbows rose up, a sure sign his strength had given out.

'He's falling, you've got to jump,' I said quietly.

'Alex!' she called. 'Get your foot up, then you'll make it!'

I grabbed hold of her harness with both hands.

'What the fuck are you doing?' she snarled, half turning.

Alex screamed. And fell. I threw Victoria off the shelf. Her short shriek drowned out Alex's longer howl. But my logic was simple: I had to get her lower as quickly as possible so that her body weight could stop his fall before he hit the ground.

The rope tensed, and then suddenly all was silence. The very wind itself seemed to be holding its breath.

I looked up.

Alex was hanging in the rope some way up the rock face. The hook had held him after all. OK, so today I didn't save anybody's life. I stepped to the edge of the ledge and looked down. Victoria Hässel was dangling on her harness two metres below me and staring up, her eyes dark with shock.

'Sorry,' I said.

'Thanks,' I said to Victoria as she poured coffee from a flask into two plastic cups and handed one to me.

She had sent Alex to join another team while she and I stayed sitting on the ledge.

'I'm the one who should say thanks.'

'For what? The hook held the rope, so it would have worked out all right anyway. And you banged your knee.'

'But you did the right thing.' She gave a crooked smile. 'So you're a climber?'

'Was,' I said. 'Haven't touched stone in almost forty years. Now tell me what I need to know. Franz Schmid rang you eight times that night after he and his brother Julian had quarrelled. The next day Julian was missing. What did Franz want?'

'I don't know. To arrange a climb maybe.'

'You never rang back. But you rang Julian's phone. Why?'

She nodded slowly. 'I called just to make sure people hadn't forgotten the most obvious option, that Julian might be somewhere and have his phone with him. What do you think has happened?' she asked. 'Did Julian go for a swim and get into trouble? Maybe because of the concussion he suffered in the bar?'

I realised she was testing me. That my reply would decide hers.

'I don't think so,' I said. 'I think Franz killed him.'

She looked less shocked than she should have done if she knew nothing.

'Well?' I said.

She looked around. The other rope team was far away, out of earshot. 'I saw Franz come home that evening. I was sitting on the balcony of my room on the other side of the road. I saw Franz get out of the car alone. Julian wasn't with him

37

and Franz was carrying something, it looked like clothes. I think he knew that I saw him and that's why he rang. He wanted to explain.'

'You didn't want to hear that?'

She sighed. 'I thought that if Julian wasn't found, or he was found dead, then I would come and tell you. Before, it would look as if I was accusing Franz of a crime. We're a group of climbers who are friends. We trust one another every day with our lives. I might have ruined all that.'

'I understand.'

'Fuck!'

I followed her gaze down. A person was on his way up the track.

'It's Franz,' she said, standing up and waving.

I peered down. 'Are you sure?'

'You can tell by the gay rights hat.'

Gay rights. The rainbow flag, not the Rastafarian. 'I thought he was hetero,' I said.

'You know you can support other people's rights besides your own?'

'And Franz Schmid does?'

'Don't know,' she said. 'But he follows St Pauli and the Bundesliga.'

'Sorry?'

'Football. His grandparents come from my city, Hamburg, and we've got two rival clubs.

38

There's HSV, which is the big, friendly and straight rich club that Julian and I support. Then you've got the angry little lefty club St Pauli, with a skull and crossbones badge, who openly support gay rights and everything else that upsets the Hamburg middle class. That seems to attract Franz.'

The figure down below had stopped and was looking up at us. I was expecting an explanation for the text message to Helena that said he had killed Julian. Perhaps that he had wanted to get Helena's attention before telling her he had stretched the truth, that all he'd done was hit his brother with a billiard ball. But seeing me with Victoria, he knew that wouldn't be enough.

The figure was moving again, heading downhill. 'He probably thinks it's too windy,' said Victoria.

'Yes,' I said.

Let him run. He wasn't going anywhere.

I was still at the police station when Franz Schmid rang just before midnight.

'Where are you?' I asked, and signalled to George that I had him on the line. 'You haven't answered my calls.'

'Signal's weak,' said Franz.

I had called the public prosecutor in Athens, and he had issued an arrest warrant for Franz Schmid.

'I paid a visit to Helena's restaurant,' said Franz. 'But her father said I couldn't see her. Does that have anything to do with you?'

'Yes.'

'I told her father that I want to marry Helena.'

'We know that. He called us.'

'Did he tell you he gave me a letter from Helena?'

'Yes.'

'You want to hear what she says?' Franz started to read without waiting for a reply:

' "Dear Franz. Maybe for everyone there is one person in this life who is meant just for us. You and I were never meant for each other, but I pray to God that you haven't killed Julian. Now that I know that he's the one for me, I ask you on bended knees: if it is within your power, save Julian. Helena."

'You seem to have made her think that I might have killed him. Do you realise you are ruining my life? I love Helena more than my own self. I just can't imagine a life without her.'

I listened. Though the wind was crackling in his phone I could hear waves.

'The best thing now would be for you to hand

yourself in to us, Franz. If you are innocent, it would be in your own best interests.'

'And if I'm guilty?'

'Then it will still be in your best interests. You can't get away. You're on an island.'

In the silence that followed I listened to the waves.

'Julian isn't innocent either,' said Franz.

I exchanged a look with George. We had both heard it. He had said is, not was. But I have heard several killers refer to their victims as though they were still alive. I know that a dead man can always be there with his killer.

'Julian lied. He claimed he'd been in touch with Helena, had told her everything, and that the two of them were in love. He wanted me to give her up without a fight. I know that Julian is a liar and a womaniser, that he'll stab you in the back to get what he wants, but this time he made me so angry. So angry, you have no idea how it feels . . .'

I didn't respond.

'Julian robbed me of the best thing I ever had,' said Franz. 'He was always the one who got them. We were born identical, but he had something I didn't. He was given light and I got darkness. And he had to have even her . . .'

The waves weren't breaking in the same brutal

way as they broke against the rocks outside my hotel. The sound was more long-drawn-out. The waves rolled more gently. Franz Schmid was on a beach.

'So I sentenced him,' he said. 'Not to death, but to life in prison. Isn't that fair punishment for ruining a life? I'm letting Julian rot in his own little love-prison. And I've thrown the key away. Although with the kind of life he has now, he won't last long.'

'Where is he, Franz?'

'What you said about me not being able to get away isn't correct. I'm about to fly out of here on flight nine nineteen, so farewell, Nikos Balli.'

'Franz, tell us where – Franz? Franz!'

The car that Franz Schmid had rented was found the next morning. It was parked by a sandy beach midway between Pothia and Massouri. Footprints led from the driver's side directly into the sea – and inside the car we found Franz Schmid's clothes, the rainbow-patterned St Pauli cap and a jacket with his phone and wallet.

George and I stood in the wind and watched the divers struggling against the waves. At the southern end of the beach they washed up against sloping rocks which, further inland, reared up in a yellow-brown limestone wall.

Franz could have come ashore on those rocks, left no footprints and got away. On flight nine nineteen? What did that mean? To get to the airport he would have had to return to the road or climb straight up that wall.

Without a rope.

Free solo.

I couldn't help it; I closed my eyes and saw Trevor fall. Then I opened them again quickly so as not to see him hit the ground.

'We found this in the shallows.'

George and I turned. It was one of the divers. He was holding up a gun. George took it. 'Looks old.'

'Luger, Second World War,' I said and took the gun from him. There was no rust and it was still well oiled, so it couldn't have been lying long in the sea. I took out the magazine and handed it to George. 'Eight if it's full.'

George squeezed out the bullets. 'Seven,' he said.

I nodded and felt an infinite sadness come over me.

'Flight nine nineteen,' I said.

'What?'

'That's the calibre of those bullets you're holding.'

*

When I rang my chief in the Homicide Department with my report, he told me journalists were in Kos waiting for the weather to calm down enough for a boat to take them to Kalymnos.

I headed back to my hotel and ordered a bottle of ouzo for my room.

After I'd drunk half the bottle I went down to the bar so as not to drink the rest. Victoria Hässel was sitting at a table with some other climbers. I sat at the bar and ordered a beer.

'Excuse me?'

British accent. I half turned. A man, smiling, check shirt, white hair but in good shape for his age, around sixty. I'd seen several like him here, English climbers of the old school. They grew up climbing in the Peak District, where the routes were graded not only by how hard they were to climb but also by how great the danger to life was.

'Do you remember me?' said the man. 'We were in the same rope team near Sheffield. Must have been in '85 or '86.'

I shook my head.

'Come on,' he said with a laugh. 'I can't recall your name but I remember you were climbing with Trevor Biggs, a local lad. And that French girl who just flew up those slopes that the rest of us had such a struggle with.' His face suddenly became serious as if he'd just thought of something. 'Bloody bad luck about Trevor, by the way.'

'I think you're getting me mixed up with someone else, sir.'

For a moment the Englishman stood there with an expression of mild surprise on his face. Then he nodded slowly. 'My apologies.'

I turned back to the bar and saw in the mirror that he sat down with his climbing friends and their climbing wives. My gaze moved on and met Victoria Hässel's.

She was dressed in the climber's evening outfit: clean climbing clothes. Her hair, which had earlier been hidden under her cap, was blonde, long and flowing. She held my gaze.

I saw that she was on the point of standing up, but I was ahead of her. I slipped off the bar stool and left. Back in my room I locked the door.

'The forecast is for the wind to drop,' said George and poured a coffee for me. 'You'll probably be able to make it over to Kos tomorrow.'

Christine and one of the constables joined us. 'You were right, George,' she said. 'Schmid bought the Luger from Marinetti. He says Franz was in the shop the day before Julian was reported missing. He bought the Luger and a pair of Italian handcuffs left over from the war. Marinetti swears, of course, that he thought the Luger had been made harmless.'

George nodded and looked pleased. When I'd wondered how Franz had managed to carry a handgun on the plane from California, George had suggested we check Marinetti's antique shop in Pothia.

For the rest of the day I wandered along narrow paths on the mountain on the southern side of the beach where we had found Franz Schmid's car.

I noticed an unusually broad overhang on the high, limestone wall. I saw a line running from a cleared belay station, the point on a rope from which climbers can hang and move their climbing partner. Here and there light from a metal glue-in bolt caught the sunlight. Because of the overhang I couldn't quite locate the anchor, and because the mountains fell directly into the sea right next to the path, I was unable to step any further out. But it had to be a long route, at least forty metres.

I looked down fifty or sixty metres to where the waves broke against the rocks. What a beautiful route it was! My brain began to imagine the climbing movements the holds would require.

My muscles glowed with pleasure as my brain recalled climbing. I could see no other routes nearby and guessed that most climbers thought it was a long way to travel just to climb one route, even though it was amazing. But I would have done it, even if it was the last route in my life.

That imaginary climb was still thrilling me in the evening. I had ordered another bottle of ouzo to my room. The wind had eased off and I could hear music coming from the bar. I guessed Victoria Hässel would be there. I sat there. It was ten o'clock, and I had drunk enough to be able to go to bed . . .

On waking the next day I threw open the window. The sea was blue, no trace of white, and no longer raging waves. Tired. Like me. I called reception.

The ferry was running again, said the receptionist. Should he order a taxi for me?

I closed my eyes. 'No taxi. Two bottles of ouzo. Have them sent up,' I said.

I drank slowly but steadily. When darkness fell I went down into the bar. As I had expected, Victoria Hässel was sitting there.

I met Monique in Oxford. She was studying literature and history, like me. But she was in the year above so we didn't go to the same lectures. But in places like that the foreigners are drawn together. I plucked up the courage to ask her out for a beer.

She made a face. 'It'll have to be a Guinness.'

'You like Guinness?'

'Probably not, I hate beer. But if we have to drink beer, then it's got to be Guinness. It's supposed to be the worst of the lot, but I promise I'll be more positive than I sound.'

Monique's logic was that everything ought to be tried: ideas, literature, music, food and drink. And me, I thought later. For we were so different. Monique was the sweetest girl I had ever met, kind to everyone. She was so unaffected by her upper-class background, her intelligence and flawless beauty that you had to like her in spite of it all.

When she looked at *you*, then of course there was no option but to fall head over heels in love. She treated the many men who chased after her with a mixture of tactful concern and mild rejection. And she was a virgin by choice, was saving herself for the right man.

With me it was the other way round. I despised my impure desires but couldn't resist them and my dark curls and brown eyes were attractive to girls. Though I think it was more than my looks that caused them to open both their hearts and bedroom doors to me – it was my ability to listen.

For me, who lived and breathed for all stories save my own, it was easy to listen to young women talk about their privileged childhoods, their problems with their mothers, their most recent unhappy love stories.

Afterwards many of them wanted to have sex with me, especially if I had hardly opened my mouth. But these sexual encounters only added to my self-contempt. These girls went to bed with me because my silence meant that they could imagine me in whatever way they wanted. I had everything to lose by revealing who I was: a stud devoid of self-confidence. And before long they noticed how my gloom shut off the light in the room, so they had to get out. I can't blame them.

With Monique all that changed. From the moment we helped each other drink that first nasty-tasting Guinness we had conversations, with the focus on *we*. We talked about matters outside ourselves, like the effects of poverty. Talked of books we'd read or not read, books we ought to read because they were good. Or bad but useful. And we argued over them.

The sparks could really fly, and it was after

one such furious argument that she, late one night and after a few glasses of wine, took a swipe at me, and then put her arms around me. And for the first time we kissed.

The next day she gave me a choice. If I wouldn't be her boyfriend then we couldn't go on meeting. It wasn't because she was desperate or in love with me, but it would mean that we would both be faithful sexually. For her this was vital, because she was frightened of sexual diseases. So afraid, in fact, that there was a fair chance the fear would spoil and shorten her life sooner than any sexual disease. I accepted her rule.

It was Monique who introduced me to climbing.

In fact in England there isn't much climbing, and certainly not around Oxford. But my fellow Led Zeppelin fan, Trevor Biggs, the slightly chubby, good-natured, red-haired son of a factory worker from Sheffield who had the room next to mine, told me of friends who climbed in the Peak District, close to his home town.

Trevor, with his outgoing manner and warm sense of humour, attracted people – guys as well as girls – who would join us at our table. Often the girls, after a time, focused on me. Trevor owned a run-down Toyota HiAce van, the special feature of which was that it had seat warmers. When I suggested that he could combine climbing with visits to his parents and share the petrol costs with two others, he went for the idea immediately.

That was the start of three years of weekend trips and climbing.

In that first year I became better than Trevor, perhaps because I was trying to impress Monique. She was far better at climbing than us. That small, neat body flew up the walls with the balance and footwork of a ballet dancer.

She understood climbing in a way that Trevor and I could only dream of. It was Monique's advice, her support and her ability to share in our joys and minor triumphs that kept me and Trevor going. And the sound of her sparkling, happy laughter echoing between the rock faces, because Trevor or I had once again fallen and dangled at the end of a rope, cursing.

In our second year I realised Trevor had begun to take climbing seriously. I had fixed a fingerboard above the door to strengthen my fingers. Now, quite often, I would see Trevor dangling there. And when it became so hot on those Peak District rock faces that Trevor and I pulled off our T-shirts, I could see that all the fat was gone from his formerly chubby upper body. Muscles rippled like steel cables under his skin. There was no doubt that the competition between Trevor and me had grown much more even. Because that's what it had become, a competition.

It was also around this time that I began partying a little too much. Meaning I did too much drinking and the mix of a lot of climbing, a lot of Monique and a lot of 'partying' began to affect my studies. Monique was the first to point it out, and this became our first quarrel. Which I won. Or at least, she was crying when she left because I'd got the last word. Next day I said sorry and promised to party less and study more.

For a while I kept that promise. I even didn't go on a weekend in the Peak District to stay in Oxford and catch up on my studies. It was tough, but the exam was coming soon, and I knew my father was expecting results as good as my older brother's. All the same, I envied Monique and Trevor their days off.

I went on putting my studies first, so much so that at one point Monique complained. It pleased me, but it was a strange pleasure, and had an even stranger side effect. From the start I felt Monique had more power over me than I had over her. It was something I accepted, believing that she was a greater catch for me than I was for her. So I came out on top there too.

What was interesting was that the less time I spent with her, the more that seemed to even out the balance of power between us. So I buried myself even deeper in my studies, and on the day of the exam I knew that what I had handed in would make not just my tutor and father proud, but Monique too.

I bought a bottle of champagne and ran to her room on the first floor of her student house. Led Zeppelin's 'Whole Lotta Love' was playing so loudly when I knocked that she didn't hear me. I was thrilled because I had given her that record, and if there was anything I felt at that moment it was a whole lotta love. I ran round to the back. Even with the bottle of champagne in one hand, I easily climbed the tree that was outside her window.

Once I was high enough to see inside I waved the bottle. I was about to call her name and tell her I loved her, but the words stuck in my throat. Monique was always very vocal when we made love, and the walls between the rooms so thin we used to play music to cover the sounds.

I saw Monique, but she didn't see me. Her eyes were closed.

Trevor didn't see me either because he had his

back to me. That now muscular back. His hips were pumping up and down almost in time to 'Whole Lotta Love'.

I was in a trance until I heard a crash and, looking down, saw the champagne bottle smashed on the path below. I slid down the tree and I ran.

I bought two bottles of Johnnie Walker, locked myself in my room and began to drink.

It was dark outside when Monique knocked on my door. I called out that I was in bed, ill. Could it wait until tomorrow? She said there was something she had to talk to me about, but I said I didn't want to take the chance of her catching what I had. Terrified of infection as she was, she left.

Trevor knocked on my door too. He asked if there was anything I needed. I whispered 'a friend', turned over in bed and called 'No thanks'.

'Hope you'll be better for our climbing trip on Friday,' said Trevor.

Friday. That gave me three days. Three days to dive down into a darkness I didn't even know existed. Three days in the grip of jealousy. Each time I breathed out it tightened its grip a little more, made it harder to breathe in fresh air. Because that's what jealousy is.

Over those three days I began to think thoughts I had no idea were inside me. And I saw the jealousy that filled me with wild visions of revenge, that sent thrilling shivers through my body and needed only another swig of whisky to keep going.

When Friday came and I rose as though from the dead, I was no longer the same Nikos Balli. No one could see it, not even Trevor and Monique when I greeted them at lunch as though nothing had happened. I just said the weather forecast looked great, that we would have a fantastic weekend.

As we ate I listened to a couple of girls on the other side of the table who were talking about a friend's new boyfriend. I listened to the words they chose, the slightly too pleased response when one spoke coldly of their mutual friend. I listened to the anger that made the sentences biting. They were jealous.

It was so simple. No, I was no longer the same. I had been somewhere. I had seen things there. Seen and learned. I had become the Jealousy Man.

'Pretty sad story that,' said Victoria Hässel as she pulled on her panties and started looking round for the rest of her clothes. 'Did the two of them become a couple?'

'No,' I said. I turned in the bed and lifted an almost empty bottle of ouzo from the bedside table and filled the dram glass. 'It was Monique's last year and her final exam was just a few days away. She didn't do very well, and after that she went home to France, and neither Trevor nor I ever saw her again. She married a Frenchman, had kids, and as far as I know lives somewhere in Brittany.'

'And you – who studied literature and history – you became a policeman?'

I shrugged. 'I had a year left at Oxford, but when I went back for the autumn the partying thing got out of hand again.'

'Broken heart?'

'Maybe. Whatever, the only thing that seemed to matter was to keep getting smashed. Once I even thought of flight nine nineteen.'

'Sorry? What?'

'When things were at their worst I would squeeze this stone I had picked up in the Peak District.' I held up a clenched fist to show what I meant. 'I focused on moving the pain into the stone, letting it suck it all out.'

'Did that help?'

'At least I didn't take flight nine nineteen.' I emptied the glass. 'Instead I dropped out in the middle of the term and took a flight to Athens.

Worked for a while in my father's firm, and then enrolled at the Police Academy. My father thought it was some kind of delayed teenage rebellion. But I knew I had been given something, a gift, or a curse, that might be of some use to me. And the rules and training at the Academy helped keep me away from . . .' I nodded towards the bottle of ouzo.

Victoria Hässel buttoned up her climbing pants, came and kissed me on my high forehead.

'Going climbing now. Adio.'

'Adio, Victoria.'

George picked me up an hour before my flight left.

'Better now?' he asked as I got into the car.

I rubbed my face.

'Yes,' I said, and it was true, I didn't feel at all bad. I had drunk myself clear. For a while, the clouds were gone. I asked him to drive slowly. I wanted to enjoy my last view of Kalymnos. It really was lovely.

When we reached the airport, George parked and we sat in his car waiting for the plane to land.

We sat in silence and looked out on Paleochora, the town made of stone.

'I told you that people from Kalymnos used to hide out there in the old days,' said George.

'Sieges could last for months. They had to sneak out at night to fetch water from hidden wells. They say children were born up there. But it was a prison, no question about it.'

A swishing in the air above us. A swishing through my head. The plane and the thought arrived at the same moment.

'The prison of love,' I said.

'What?'

'Both Franz and Julian had dates with Helena in Paleochora. Franz said he had sentenced his brother to life in his own prison of love. That could mean . . .'

The brief roaring of the propellers drowned out my words as the plane landed, but George had already understood.

'I guess this means,' he said, 'that you won't be taking the plane to Athens after all?'

'Call Christine. Tell her to bring Odin with her.'

Christine's golden retriever had been born with only one working eye and, according to George, was a good tracker.

From a distance Paleochora looked like a ghost town. Grey-black and lifeless. But close up, as happens in murder cases too, the details and colours began to appear. And the smell.

George and I hurried through the ruins

58

towards one of the houses that was still more or less intact. Christine was standing in the doorway. She had been the first to arrive, along with two members of the mountain rescue team, and we'd been talking over the radios. Christine pointed us towards what was probably Paleochora's only cellar.

The first thing that struck me when George and I bent down and entered the low-ceilinged room, and before my eyes had adapted to the dark, was the stench.

Julian Schmid gradually took shape in front of me, his naked body partly covered by a dirty woollen blanket. One of the mountain rescue men was squatting beside him, but there was little he could do. Julian's arms reached stiffly above his head. His hands were fastened by handcuffs to an iron bolt in the stone wall.

'Teodore's bringing something to cut the handcuffs,' whispered George, as though this was a church service.

I looked at the floor, at a pool of shit, vomit and urine. That was the source of the smell.

The man on the floor coughed. 'Water,' he whispered.

The mountain rescue team had already given him all they had, so I pressed my bottle against the dry lips. It was like seeing a half-dead mirror image of Franz but Julian Schmid seemed thinner than his twin brother. He had a large blue mark on his forehead, perhaps from that billiard ball, and his voice sounded different.

'Franz?' whispered Julian.

'He's disappeared,' I said.

'And Helena?'

'Safe.'

'Can one of you tell her? That I'm OK?'

George and I exchanged glances. I nodded to Julian.

'Thank you,' he said, and drank again. And tears began to trickle from his eyes, as though the water was running straight through his head. 'He didn't mean it.'

'What?'

'Franz. He just went crazy. It sometimes happens to him.'

'I think that, deep down, Franz wanted you to be found,' I said quietly.

'You think so?' said Julian.

I knew then that he knew Franz was dead. And that I would tell him what he needed to hear, if he was ever to be whole again.

'He regretted it,' I said. 'He told me that you were here. He wanted me to rescue you. He had no way of knowing that I would take time to understand.'

'It hurts so much,' he said.

'I know,' I said.

'What can you do?'

I looked around. I picked up a grey stone from the ground and pressed it into his hands. 'You squeeze that. Imagine that it's drawing all the pain out of you.'

When I arrived at the hospital in Pothia, Helena was by the bedside and holding Julian's hand. He was already looking better, and Helena seemed to think it was my razor-sharp brain that had saved him. And when I asked for a few words alone with Julian, she grabbed my hand and kissed it before she left us.

Julian's account of events was pretty much what I had been expecting. On the way to hospital after the fight in the bar the quarrel with Franz flared up again.

'I lied,' said Julian. 'I said I had told Helena everything – all about my pretending to be Franz. And that she forgave me and told me she loved me. I thought I would call Helena afterwards, and the result would be the same. But Franz screamed that it was a lie. He pulled the car in to the side of the road and took out a pistol. I had never seen him like that before, never so . . . crazy.'

Julian's eyes were bright. 'But I don't blame

him. I stole Helena. I betrayed them both. I would have done the same to him. No, I would have killed him. Instead he forced me to drive up to Paleochora with a gun in my back.'

'And then he left you to die?'

'He said I could stay there until I rotted. I was terrified, but I was more afraid for Helena than myself. Because he always came back.'

'What do you mean?'

'When we used to fight as kids, sometimes he would lock me up in a room, or a cupboard. Once it was a chest and he said I would die there. But he always came back. And I was certain the same thing would happen this time too. Right up until . . .' He looked at me. 'Well, I simply knew something had happened to Franz. And I began to think I really was going to die there. You saved me, Mr Balli. I'll be forever in your debt.' Julian pushed a hand from under the duvet and took mine. I felt the stone I had given him pressed into my palm. 'In case you too should ever feel pain,' he said.

It was after midnight by the time I let myself into my flat.

'I'm home,' I called into the dark, and went to the kitchen area of the big, open-plan room with its glass walls and its views of Kolonaki.

I took out the little box I had in my pocket and looked at the grey stone lying inside, like a jewel in a jeweller's box.

I got a glass, opened the fridge, and the light fell across the wooden floor and reached across to the bookshelves and the heavy teak writing desk with the big Apple screen.

All bought with money I inherited, not my police salary.

I filled the glass with the fresh juice my house-keeper makes, crossed to the computer and touched the keyboard. A big picture of three young people in front of a rock face in the Peak District appeared.

I kissed my finger and placed it on the cheek of the girl between the two boys on the screen, and said that now I was off to bed.

In the bedroom I put the grey stone on the shelf above the bed, next to the other stone that lay there. The bed was so big and empty. The silk sheets looked so chilly that, as I lay down, I had the feeling I was about to swim out to sea.

Two weeks later I got a phone call from George Kostopoulos.

'A body's been found in the sea not far from where Franz disappeared,' he said. 'Or actually, on the rocks where the waves break. People don't go there much, but it looks as though someone has started climbing along a route fifty or sixty metres above the rocks and fallen. A climber called it in.'

'I know where it is,' I said. 'Has the body been identified?'

'Not yet. It's so badly smashed up it's hard even to see that it's human. But there's a bullet hole in the skull. I've sent a DNA sample from the body. I was just wondering . . .'

'Yeah?'

'If it matches the DNA from the saliva we took from Franz Schmid's water glass, what do we say?'

'We say we made a positive identification.'

'But remember, we got that DNA outside of the rules.'

'Oh? As far as I remember we asked Franz Schmid and he gave it to us of his own free will.'

It was silent at the other end. 'Is that the way . . .' he began.

'Yes,' I said. 'That's the way we do it in Athens.'

The results arrived three days later.

The DNA from the human remains on the rocks matched that given to detectives by Franz Schmid.

I thought about that climbing route out there

south of the beach. I had found out that the route was called Where Eagles Dare, grade 7b. Even in a photo it looked fantastic. If I was ever going to get in shape to climb it, I would need to train and lose a few kilos. And for me to have time for that, people would either have to take a break from killing each other, or I would have to take a break. A long one.

Five Years Later

I looked out of the plane window. The island beneath was unchanged: a yellow block of limestone. But the skies were clouded over.

The weather was less stable in spring, the taxi driver told me on my way into Emporio. I smiled as I looked at the oleander bushes in full bloom on the hillsides and breathed in the scent of thyme.

Helena and Julian were standing on the steps of the restaurant with little Ferdinand as I got out of the taxi. Julian smiled broadly while Helena hugged me as though she would never let go. We had sent emails regularly, by which I mean she told me how things were going and I read her messages. Read the way I listened, and replied briefly, mostly follow-up questions, as I often did when chatting to people.

It hadn't been easy in the beginning, she wrote. Julian was affected by what had happened. After the joy of being rescued and being back with her he became dark and closed-off. He was different from the man she had fallen in love with. And he spoke so much of his brother. He made excuses for Franz. It seemed important to Julian that Franz wasn't evil, that he had simply been very, very much in love.

It got so bad that she was thinking about leaving him, until something happened that changed everything: she became pregnant.

And from that day on, it was as though Julian had woken up and become again the Julian she could scarcely remember from the single night they had spent together before he went missing. Happy, good, kind, warm, loving. He had cried like a child himself when Ferdinand was born. Like his father, the boy radiated love.

'Like some kind of heater,' she wrote. 'And when the winter storms batter Kalymnos you couldn't wish for anything better.'

'So you think you're ready for Where Eagles Dare,' said a smiling Julian once we were seated at lunch in the restaurant.

'I don't know,' I said. 'But I've done a little climbing on the crags around Athens.'

'Then we'll start out early tomorrow,' he said.

'It's a very long route,' I said. 'Forty metres.'

'No problem, I have an eighty-metre rope.'

'Excellent.'

The ringtone on his phone played. He was about to take the call when he stopped and looked at me.

'You look so pale, Nikos? Is everything OK?'

'Of course,' I lied, and managed to return his smile. I could feel the sweat breaking out all over my body. 'Take the call.'

He gave me a long, searching look, then picked up the phone and finally the tune 'Whole Lotta Love' stopped playing. The song not only took me forty years back in time, to a tree in a yard in Oxford, it actually made me feel physically ill.

'Didn't you like the music?' Julian asked once his call was finished.

'It's a long story,' I said, and laughed now that I had had time to compose myself. 'But I thought you didn't like Led Zeppelin. I seem to remember you had something a bit softer on your phone. Ed something. Ed Cheap. Ed Sheep . . .'

'Ed Sheeran!' cried Helena.

'That's it,' I said.

'I love Sheeran,' said Helena.

'How about you, Julian?'

Julian Schmid raised his glass of water. 'It's quite possible to like both Zeppelin and Sheeran.'

He drank for a long time without taking his eyes off me.

'I just thought of something,' he said when finally he put his glass down. 'The weather forecast for tomorrow says there might be rain, so why don't we head out there now? You're here for such a short time and this way we can be sure you'll be able to have a crack at it before you have to leave.'

We finished the meal and I went up to my room to get ready. As I packed my climbing gear, through the window I could see Julian playing with Ferdinand. The boy ran laughing around his father, and each time Julian grabbed hold of him and swung him round the boy shrieked with joy.

'Excited?' asked Julian as we parked after our silent drive out to the spot where we had found Franz's car.

I nodded. The beach looked different today. No sun.

After a brisk twenty-minute walk we were out on the point and looking up at Where Eagles Dare. It looked more frightening with the steel-grey clouds hanging over it. We put on our climbing harnesses. I attached myself to the rope and pulled on the old, comfortable climbing shoes I had used in the Peak District. Instead of stepping the two paces to the wall, I walked out to the edge of the path and looked down.

'That's where they found him,' I said, nodding down towards the breakers. Their sound reached up to us. 'But you already knew that.'

'How long have you known?' said the voice behind me.

'Known what?'

I turned to face him. He was pale. Maybe it was just the light, but for a moment his almost white skin made me think of Trevor. But nowadays I think quite often of Trevor.

'Nothing,' he said, his face and voice blank as he threaded the rope through the manual brake fastened to his halter. 'You're in, the carabiner is fastened, the rope is long enough, and your knot looks fine.'

I nodded. I placed one foot in the overhanging wall and gripped into the first handhold, I tensed my body and got my other foot up.

The first ten metres of the climb were fine. I moved easily. And at the crux, the hardest point of the route, I felt the flow, that time when there's no need to think, when the hands and feet seem to make the moves all by themselves. Reaching the top, I clipped the rope into the anchor with a sense of contentment that was deep and calm.

The climb had been magical. I turned to take in the view. According to George, on a clear day you could see the coast of Turkey, but today I saw only the sea, myself, the route. And the rope that ran down to the man I had saved, and who would save me.

'Ready!' I shouted. 'You can lower me down!'

I sank down through the still, heavy afternoon

air. Daylight was already fading when, after a few metres, I saw the dark section on the yellow rope passing beside me on its way up to the anchor.

The midpoint marker.

'The rope's too short!' I shouted.

But Julian went on letting out the rope, faster now.

I looked down and I could see now that there was no knot in the loose end of the rope.

'Julian!' I shouted. I was so close to him I could see the deadness in his face. He was going to kill me. There were only a few seconds before the end of the rope would slide through the brake, and I would fall.

'Franz!'

My descent stopped. I swayed in empty air. If the rope passed through the brake I would fall past Julian, sixty metres down to the rocks where the waves frothed like the contents of a smashed champagne bottle.

'Looks like the rope isn't eighty metres after all,' said Julian. 'Sorry.' He didn't look as if he was sorry.

It was his choice now. His game was near its end. That end was twenty centimetres below the brake and his hand. It wasn't hard for him to hold me there. But he couldn't do it for ever. And, when he let go, it wouldn't look like a murder, but like a common climbing accident: the rope was too short.

We studied each other. Him on the track and me dangling over the abyss.

'Paradox,' he said. 'That's a Greek word, isn't it? Like when Ferdinand is afraid of the dark when it's bedtime, and he wants Daddy to tell him fairy stories until he's asleep. But he insists that they're scary stories. Isn't that a paradox?'

'Perhaps,' I said.

'In any case, you can see the darkness coming, so maybe you should tell a scary story now, Nikos. And then maybe you and I won't be so afraid.'

I looked down. A fall of sixty metres doesn't take long. I had seen that close up. The stillness and the lack of drama had been the most striking thing, in the seconds after he hit the ground.

It had turned cold, and yet I could feel the sweat running like melting wax. I had not planned to expose the fake Julian in this way, with my life literally in his hands. On the other hand, it made everything easier.

'OK,' I said. 'Are you ready?'

'I'm ready.'

'Once upon a time . . .' I took a deep breath. 'Once upon a time there was a man named Franz who was so jealous that he killed his twin brother Julian, so that he could have the lovely

Helena all to himself. He took his brother down to a beach, shot him in the head and threw the body into the sea.

'But when Franz realised that Helena loved only Julian, and that she didn't want Franz, Franz arranged things in such a way that it looked as though it was him and not Julian who had ended up with a bullet through the head.

'Afterwards he chained himself up in a cellar and when he was found he pretended to be Julian, and everyone believed him. And so Franz did get his Helena, and they all lived happily ever after. Will that do?'

He shook his head. 'You have no proof.'

'What makes you think that?'

'With proof I would have been arrested a long time ago. And you've left the police force. So what's this visit all about? Is this the old man come to pursue the case that won't give him any peace, because he no longer feels certain he found out the truth?'

'It's true that I'm not at peace,' I said. 'Though it's not about this case. But it is not true that I'm here in search of proof, because I already have proof.'

'You're lying.' The knuckles of the hand holding the rope whitened.

'No,' I said. 'When the DNA from the body

in the sea matched what we got from Franz during the interrogation, everybody thought that wrapped things up. But of course identical twins have the same DNA profile. So the body could just as well have been Julian as Franz.'

'So what? That's not proof.'

'Correct. I didn't get my proof until I was sent the fingerprints that you, Franz, left on the glass you drank from at the police station in Pothia. I compared them with the prints I had at home in Athens.'

'Athens?'

'On the stone you gave me at the hospital. Yes, paradox is Greek, and the paradox here is that even though twins have identical DNA, their fingerprints are not identical.'

'That's not true. We compared fingerprints, and they were the same.'

'*Almost* the same. Fingerprints are affected by your place in the womb. By the position each baby lies in, and by the difference in the lengths of the umbilical cords. That causes a difference in the access to food which, again, affects how quickly the fingers grow.

'By the time your fingerprints are fully formed, between week thirteen and nineteen of the pregnancy, small differences can be seen on close examination. I gave them a close examination.

And guess what? The fingerprints on the stone I got from you at the hospital when you were claiming to be Julian, and on the glass that you, Franz, drank from at the police station, were identical.'

Maybe it was just the onset of darkness, but it seemed to me I could see Franz emerge, see him step out of the role he had been playing all these years.

'And you are the only one who knows this?' he said quietly.

'Correct.'

From out at sea came the single, pained cry of a gull.

I could see Franz loosening his hold, saw the yellow-taped end slide up towards his hand.

'You must have had clothing and shoes to get up to Paleochora,' I said. 'Where did you get rid of them?'

'In Chora,' he said. 'In a rubbish bin below the fortress walls. Along with the packaging for the drug that caused my vomiting and the laxatives I took, so that it would look as though I had been chained there for a long time before you found me. I made it up to the cellar, then I shat and puked like a pig. I really thought it wouldn't take you long to find me.'

'And of course, you didn't chain yourself to

the wall until you knew that "rescue" wasn't far away. The key to the handcuffs, where did you hide that?'

'I swallowed it.'

'And that was all you ate while you were there? No wonder you looked a good deal thinner.'

Franz Schmid laughed. 'I got a bit desperate when I realised you weren't taking the hint. I started shouting for help. Shouted myself hoarse.'

'That's why your voice was different,' I said.

'No one heard me,' said Franz.

I took a deep breath. I felt the climbing harness tighten.

'So you took over the life of your own brother.'

Franz Schmid shrugged. 'Julian and I knew each other's lives inside out. The hardest thing was the funeral back home, when my mother said she was certain that I was Franz, and that grief must have driven her mad. After the burial I left Julian's job and came back to Kalymnos.'

'And Helena . . . does she know anything?'

Franz Schmid shook his head. 'Why are you doing this?' he asked. 'You give me a rope and tie yourself to the other end and tell me that if I kill you no one will know anything.'

'Let me ask you, Franz, isn't it terrible to have to bear the weight of this alone?'

He didn't reply.

'If you kill me now, you'll still be alone. Is that what you want?'

'You leave me with no choice, Nikos.'

'A man always has a choice.'

'When it comes to his own life maybe. But I have a family. I love them, they love me, and I will make any sacrifice for them. Peace in my soul. Your life. Do you really think that's so strange?'

I fell. I saw the end of the rope disappear into Franz's hand and knew it was all over. But then the harness tightened again and I swayed lightly on the stretchy rope.

'Not strange,' I said. My pulse dropped. The worst was over. I was no longer so afraid to die. 'Because that's what I've come here to offer you. Peace in your soul.'

'Not possible.'

'I know I can't give you perfect peace. After all, you killed your brother. But I can offer you peace from the fear of being exposed.'

He gave a quick laugh. 'And why aren't you going to arrest me?'

'Because I want the same thing in return.'

'The same thing?'

'Peace in my soul. It means I can't arrest you without doing the same thing to myself.'

I saw the muscles move beneath the skin of his hand. His neck muscles tensed, and he breathed more heavily. I only had seconds left to tell the story of the day that had shaped the rest of my life.

'So what plans have you got for the summer?' I asked Trevor as I raised the Thermos cup to my mouth.

Trevor, Monique and I were sitting facing each other. Behind us was a wall some twenty metres high, and in front of us a landscape of meadows. On clear days like today, from the top of the wall, you could see the smoke from the factory chimneys in Sheffield.

We had finished climbing, taking a short break before heading back. The hot cup scorched my raw fingertips, and felt slippery because I had just rubbed cream into my fingers – a women's cosmetic cream that was better for rebuilding new skin than any climbers' cream.

'Don't know,' Trevor answered.

It was difficult to get him talking today. Same with Monique. It was me – the one with the broken heart – who did the talking. Joked. Kept the spirits up. Of course I saw them swapping looks that said who's going to tell him, you or me? They were probably desperate to confess their sins, swear it would never happen again. But I didn't give them an opening.

Strangely, given my disturbed state of mind, I had climbed well. And was very relaxed, not thinking about danger. Things seemed the other way round for Trevor and Monique, Trevor especially.

'What about your summer plans?' asked Trevor. He took a bite of his sandwich.

'Work a bit for my father in Athens,' I said. 'Earn enough to visit Monique in France and finally get to say hello to her family.'

I smiled at Monique, who returned my smile stiffly.

'We'd better tell you,' said Trevor in a low voice, staring down at the ground.

I felt myself grow cold, felt my heart sink in my chest.

'I'm planning a trip to France too in the summer.'

What the hell did he mean? Weren't they going to tell me what had happened? About this slip-up that was behind them now. About Monique who had been feeling so alone because I had been neglecting her, and Trevor who had given in to a moment of weakness.

Weren't they going to tell me how sorry they felt, and promise that it would never happen again? Wasn't any of this going to come out? Trevor was going to France. Were the two of them . . . ?

I looked at Monique, but her gaze too was fixed to the ground. It dawned on me that I had been blind. But I had been blind because the two of them had put my eyes out. Something big and evil and black surged up inside me. It was as though my stomach twisted and a stinking, yellow-green spew was trying to force its way out. There was no way out; mouth, nose, ears, the sockets of my eyes, were all sewn shut. So the spew filled my head, driving out every sensible thought, surging and bursting inside me.

I could see Trevor preparing for it. For the crux, the point. He took a deep breath, his new broad shoulders and his back swelled up. That back I had seen through the window. He opened his mouth.

'You know what?' I said quickly. 'I'd like to climb one route more before we go.'

Trevor and Monique swapped confused glances. 'I . . .' Monique began.

'It shouldn't take long,' I said. 'Only Exodus.'

'Why?' said Monique. 'You've already climbed it today.'

'Because I want to climb free solo,' I said.

The two of them stared at me. The silence was

so complete we could follow the chat between a climber and his anchor a hundred metres away along the rock face. I pulled on my climbing shoes.

'Don't mess about,' said Trevor with a strained laugh.

I saw from Monique's look that she knew I wasn't messing about.

I wiped my slippery, greasy fingertips dry against my climbing trousers and walked over to the face. Exodus was a route we'd climbed dozens of times with ropes. It was easy all the way up to the crux – the most difficult point – near the end, where you need to forget your balance and throw your left hand out towards a little handhold that slopes slightly downwards. The only thing that stops you falling is the drag of your fingers on the rock.

We could see from the ground that the hand-hold was white from climbers who, directly before making that move, had dipped their hands into the pouches of chalk attached to their harness or waist, so their skin would be as dry as possible.

'Nikos . . .' Monique said, but I had already started climbing.

Ten seconds later I was high up the crag. I heard the chat further along the face suddenly stop, and I knew the other climbers had realised I was climbing without rope, with no security. I heard one of them curse. But on I climbed.

And it was fantastic. The rock. Death. It was better than all the whisky in the world. For the first time since I saw Trevor and Monique fucking I was free of pain. I was now so high that, if I fell, I would die. And that day, the more I thought about death, the easier the climbing seemed to be.

I was at the crux. All I had to do was let my body drop to the left and catch the fall with my left hand on that single, small handhold. I stopped to enjoy the moment. Enjoy their fear.

I heard a little scream from Monique and felt a lovely hollowness as I leaned and trusted myself to gravity. I threw out my left hand. Found the ledge and gripped hard. The fall was over almost before it had begun. I moved my right hand to the big hold and got my feet up on the ledge. I was safe. And felt almost immediately a strange dismay.

The other climbers, two Englishmen, had crossed over to Trevor and Monique. I heard them say the usual things: how free soloing should be banned, that climbing is about risk-management, not about challenging death. And I heard Monique defending me. Trevor said nothing.

Resting before the final few metres, I used a common climber's method: alternately turning the right hip and the left in towards the rock face, holding on with my left and then right hand as I did so. As my left hip brushed against the rock, I felt something prick me. It was the tube of women's cosmetic cream in my trouser pocket.

I held on to the rock with my right hand, and stuck my left hand into my trouser pocket. With my left side twisted towards the rock, both were hidden from those below. I unscrewed the cap, squeezed the tube and held the thick, fatty cream between two fingers. I placed my left hand back on that handhold at the crux, seemingly to adjust the position of my feet, and smeared the white cream. I wiped my hand dry on the inside of my thigh, then climbed the last few steps to the summit.

By the time I had climbed down the rear of the crag and walked round to the front, the two other climbers had gone. Clouds were moving in from the west.

'You idiot,' hissed Monique.

'I love you too,' I said and took off my shoes. 'Your turn, Trevor.'

I can only think, based on what he did, that he knew that I knew. And this would be his penance; to challenge death in the same way as I had.

'You won't make your idiotic action any less idiotic by persuading him to do something just as idiotic!' hissed Monique. There were tears in her eyes. I wondered if they were for me. For us. Or for the moral trap she and Trevor had fallen into, which was so opposed to everything she thought she stood for?

And when Monique realised I was looking behind her she turned, and saw Trevor on his way up the crag. She screamed. But Trevor was beyond the point at which he could regret it and turn back. Beyond the point at which *I* could regret it.

I could have warned him. Did I consider it? Which pain would be the greater? The one I would have to live with if Trevor had travelled to France that summer and maybe spent the rest of his life with Monique? Or the one I was fated to live with – to lose both of them anyway?

And would any of those pains have been worse than to have lived with Monique, lived a lie? Lived with her knowing that our marriage was based not on mutual love but on mutual guilt? That it was built on the gravestone of the man she had loved more than me?

I could have warned him, but I didn't.

Because back then I would have chosen the same as I would today – to live a life of lies, denial and guilt with her. And if I had known that such a thing was impossible, I would have wished that it were me who had fallen. But I didn't. I had to live on. Until today.

I remember little of the rest of that day.

What I do remember is the drive back to Oxford. It's night, and several hours since Trevor's body has been brought down. Monique and I have given our statements to the police, and we have tried to explain to Trevor's desperate mother, while his father's sobs of pain cut through the air.

I'm driving. Monique is silent. The temperature had fallen with the coming of rain, so I've turned on the seat warmers. I'm thinking that now it will all have been washed away, the proof against me on the crux. And in the warm interior Monique suddenly says she can smell perfume and turns towards me, glancing down into my lap.

'You've got something white on the inside of your thigh.'

'Chalk,' I say quickly, without taking my eyes off the road.

We drive the rest of the way in silence.

*

'You killed your best friend,' said Franz Schmid, neither shocked nor accusing. He was simply stating a fact.

'Now you know as much about me as I know about you,' I said.

He looked up at me. 'And you think that means I've nothing to fear from you. But your crime is beyond the legal limit now. You can't be punished for it.'

'Don't you think I've been punished, Franz?' I closed my eyes. It didn't really matter if he let go of the rope. I had made my confession. Naturally he couldn't forgive me. But he could – *we* could – give each other a story that said that we were not alone, not the only sinner.

It doesn't make it forgivable, but it makes it human. It turns it into a human failing. The failure is always human. And that at least makes me human. And Franz too. Did he understand that? That I had come to turn him into a human being? And myself too? That I was his rescuer, and he mine? I opened my eyes again. Looked at his hand.

By the time we headed back down it was dark and as soon as we reached the car Franz called Helena.

'We're fine, darling.' A smile spread over his

face. 'Tell him Daddy will be home soon and I'll read to him. Tell him I love you both.'

Franz put the phone down. But he didn't start the engine. 'I still don't understand it,' he said. 'I mean, you're a policeman.'

'No,' I said. 'I never was a policeman. I just worked as one. You've got to understand that in the story about me, I am you, Franz. Julian betrayed you the way Trevor betrayed me. And the disease of jealousy made killers out of both of us. Life imprisonment in Greece means you can get released on parole after sixteen years. I've served more than twice that. I wouldn't want the same thing to happen to you.'

'You can't even know whether or not I feel regret,' said Franz. 'Maybe I didn't need to confess to find peace.'

'I had another reason for coming,' I said.

'And that is?'

'You're the road I never took. I had to see it.'

'What do you mean?'

'You chose her, you chose the one who was the reason you killed your own brother. Is it possible to live with that? That's what I wanted to know. Can you live in happiness with the one you killed for in the shadow of that gravestone? I have always believed that was impossible for me.'

'And now that you've seen the other road and

know that it's possible, what are you going to do about it?'

Franz drove me to the airport two days later. We didn't talk much during those days; it was as though both of us were empty. Most of my talk had been with Helena and Ferdinand.

There was a rain storm just as we pulled up in front of the terminal, and we sat in the car to wait it out. Franz sat looking out through the windscreen as though building up the courage to say something. I was hoping it wouldn't be anything too big and dark. When he did finally begin he spoke without looking at me.

'Ferdinand asked me this morning where your children and their mother were,' said Franz. 'When I said you didn't have any, he asked me to give you this.' Franz pulled a worn little teddy bear up out of his jacket pocket and handed it to me.

His gaze met mine. We both laughed. 'And this,' he added.

It was a photograph they had evidently printed out on photo paper. It showed me swinging Ferdinand round just the same way I had seen his father do.

'Thanks,' I said.

'I think you'll make a good grandpa.'

I looked at the picture. Helena had taken it. 'Will you ever tell her? What really happened?'

'Helena?' Franz shook his head. 'In the beginning I ought to have done, of course. But now . . .' He stopped.

'But?'

He sighed. 'Sometimes I get the feeling she knows.'

'Really?'

'It's something she said once. She said she loved me, and I said I loved her. And then she asked if I loved her so much that I would have killed someone I loved only a little bit less in order to have her. Then before I could answer she kissed me and started talking about something else.'

'Who knows?' I said. 'And who needs to know?'

That evening in my home in Athens I put the teddy bear on the shelf above the bed and took down an opened envelope. It was postmarked Paris and dated two months ago. I read the letter it held one more time. Her handwriting hadn't changed after all these years.

It was late at night before I finally managed to get to sleep.

Three months later

'Thank you for a perfect day,' said Victoria Hässel and raised her wine glass. 'Who would have thought there was such good climbing to be had in Athens. And you with such powers of endurance.'

She winked to make certain I got the double meaning. Victoria had contacted me a few days after I had returned from Kalymnos, and we wrote at least once a week after that. Maybe the distance, and the fact that we had no mutual friends and didn't know each other very well made it easy for me to confide in her. Not about murder but about love. And that meant Monique.

Victoria's love life was a little richer and more varied. When she wrote that she was going to meet her latest flame, a French climber, in Sardinia, and was planning to travel via Athens, I was not sure whether it was such a good idea for us to meet. I wrote, telling her that I liked the distance, talking to a confessor who couldn't see my face.

'I can always wear a paper bag over my head,' she wrote back. 'But I won't be wearing much more than that.'

'Is your brother's flat as posh as this?' Victoria asked as I cleared the table.

'Posher and bigger.' My brother had taken over the family business because I'd become a policeman.

'Does that make you envious?'

'No. I'm . . .'

'Happy?'

'I was about to say, content.'

'Me too. So content it's almost a pity I have to travel on to Sardinia tomorrow.'

'You've got someone waiting for you, and I hear the climbing there is fantastic too.'

'You're not jealous?'

'Of the climbing, or of your boyfriend? I think it's his job to be jealous of me.'

'I was single that time in Kalymnos.'

'You told me. And I'm a lucky man who's been able to borrow you for a while.'

We took our wine glasses out onto the balcony.

'Have you come to any decision about Monique?' she asked as we looked out across Kolonaki. I had told Victoria about the letter. That Monique was now a widow and had moved to Paris. And how she had written that she thought about me a lot and wanted me to go over and meet her.

'Yes,' I said. 'I'm going over.'

'It'll be fantastic,' she said as she raised her glass.

'Well, I'm not too sure about that,' I said.

'Why not?'

'Because it's probably too late. We're different people now.'

'If you're so gloomy, why go?'

'Because I need to know where the other road leads to, the one we didn't take. Whether happiness would have been possible in the shadow of a gravestone.'

'I've no idea what you're talking about. But *is* it?'

I thought about it. Franz lied to everyone around him, all day, every day. I couldn't do that. I simply didn't have the talent or the patience. If I went to Paris, I would have to tell Monique what I did that day in the Peak District.

I walked Victoria back to her hotel. Her departure was at the crack of dawn the next day. Then I headed back home. I walked a long way round because I knew I wouldn't be able to sleep.

Maybe Monique suspected all along. Maybe the remark she made about the stain on my thigh when the seat warmers had caused the cosmetic cream to smell so strongly was just her way of letting me know. That she knew, and that she also knew that, because of her betrayal of me, in some way she shared the guilt, and that our ways must part here.

But now, late in life, it could be that we had actually found our way back to that crossroads where we had taken leave of one another. Now – if we wanted to, if we dared – we could take that other road. Me, a murderer. But I had served my time, hadn't I? I was able to feel good about Franz and about his happiness. Might I also be able to feel good about my own?

About Quick Reads

"Reading is such an important building block for success"
~ Jojo Moyes

Quick Reads are short books written
by best-selling authors.

Did you enjoy this Quick Read?

Tell us what you thought by filling in
our short survey. Scan the **QR code**
to go directly to the survey or
visit **bit.ly/QR2024**

Thanks to Penguin Random House and Hachette and to all
our publishing partners for their ongoing support.

A special thank you to Jojo Moyes for her generous donation in
2020-2022 which helped to build the future of Quick Reads.

Quick Reads is delivered by The Reading Agency, a UK charity
with a mission to get people fired up about reading, because
everything changes when you read.

www.readingagency.org.uk   @readingagency   #QuickReads

The Reading Agency Ltd. Registered number: 3904882 (England & Wales)
Registered charity number: 1085443 (England & Wales)
Registered Office: 24 Bedford Row, London, WC1R 4EH
The Reading Agency is supported using public funding by
Arts Council England.

Find your next Quick Read...

For 2024 we have selected 6 popular
Quick Reads for you to enjoy!

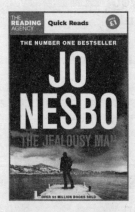

Quick Reads are available to buy in paperback or ebook and to borrow from your local library. For a complete list of titles and more information on the authors and their books visit **www.readingagency.org.uk/quickreads**

Continue your reading journey with The Reading Agency:

Reading Ahead

Challenge yourself to complete six reads by taking part in **Reading Ahead** at your local library, college or workplace: **readingahead.org.uk**

Reading
Groups
for Everyone

Join **Reading Groups for Everyone** to find a reading group and discover new books: **readinggroups.org.uk**

World Book Night

Celebrate reading on **World Book Night** every year on 23 April: **worldbooknight.org**

Summer Reading Challenge

Read with your family as part of the **Summer Reading Challenge: summerreadingchallenge.org.uk**

For more information on our work and the power of reading please visit our website: **readingagency.org.uk**

More from Quick Reads

If you enjoyed the 2024 Quick Reads please explore our 6 titles from 2023.

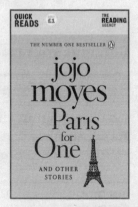

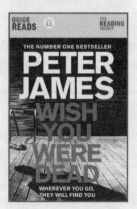

For a complete list of titles and more information on the authors and their books visit:
www.readingagency.org.uk/quickreads

About the author

Jo Nesbo is one of the world's bestselling crime writers. His books *The Leopard*, *Phantom*, *Police*, *The Son*, *The Thirst*, *Macbeth* and *Knife* have all topped the *Sunday Times* charts. He's an international number one bestseller and his books are published in 50 languages, selling over 55 million copies around the world.

1 3 5 7 9 10 8 6 4 2

Vintage is part of the Penguin Random House group of companies
whose addresses can be found at global.penguinrandomhouse.com

Penguin
Random House
UK

This Quick Reads edition published in 2024
First published in hardback by Harvill Secker in 2021
First published in Norway by H. Aschehoug & Co
(W. Nygaard), Oslo, in 2021

Published by agreement with Salomonsson Agency
English translation copyright © Robert Ferguson 2021

penguin.co.uk/vintage

Printed and bound in Great Britain by Clays Ltd, Elcograf S.p.A.

The authorised representative in the EEA is Penguin Random House
Ireland, Morrison Chambers, 32 Nassau Street, Dublin D02 YH68

A CIP catalogue record for this book
is available from the British Library

ISBN 9781529928280

Penguin Random House is committed to a sustainable future
for our business, our readers and our planet. This book is made
from Forest Stewardship Council® certified paper.

JO NESBO

KILLING MOON

A **HARRY HOLE** THRILLER

JO NESBO

THE BAT

A HARRY HOLE THRILLER

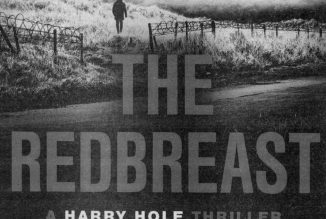

JO NESBO

THE REDBREAST

A HARRY HOLE THRILLER

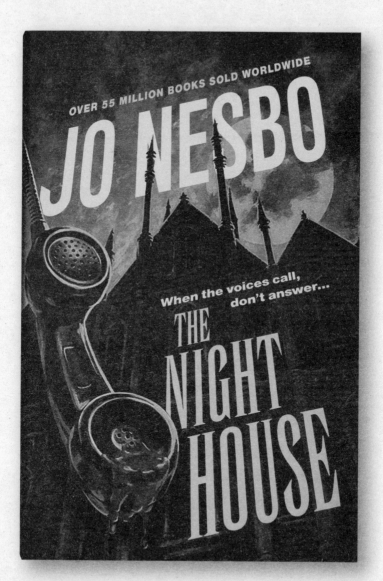

OVER 55 MILLION BOOKS SOLD WORLDWIDE

JO NESBO

When the voices call,
don't answer...

THE NIGHT HOUSE